A SNAIL'S TALE

Sarah Edwards

Happy

Best wishes

Sarah Edwards

ARTHUR H. STOCKWELL LTD
Torrs Park, Ilfracombe, Devon, EX34 8BA
Established 1898
www.ahstockwell.co.uk

First published in Great Britain, 2017

British Library Cataloguing-in-Publication Data.
A catalogue record for this book is available from the British Library.

To Gareth, Mum and Dad, for always being there – *S.E.*

ISBN 978-0-7223-4696-9
Printed in Great Britain by
Arthur H. Stockwell Ltd
Torrs Park Ilfracombe
Devon

Somewhere in a garden, not too far away,
Lived a snail with a name not so easy to say.
Omalvus was the name that belonged to this snail,
A snail who could draw with his rainbow slime trail.

He drew flowers and trees,
Ants, green grasses and bees.
All his colours were bright,
Green, pink, yellow and white.

He loved to draw
All the things he saw.
Omalvus the snail,
With his rainbow slime trail.

One day Omalvus came across a cat,
A ginger tom, big, fluffy and fat.
He slept peacefully on the ground,
His gentle purring the only sound.

The cat had a twitch and stretched his paws,
Revealing his long and sharp white claws.
Omalvus thought it would be rather nice,
To draw this big tom who was dreaming of mice.

Omalvus started with the big cat's head,
Patterned with stripes of orangey red.
His ears were pointed, alert and upright,
Listening for sounds however slight.

The snail was busy for a long while,
His face lit up with an enormous smile.
He was having such a wonderful time,
Drawing the cat with his rainbow slime.

His picture glistened in the sun,
It was the best he'd ever done.
He had drawn the cat from tail to nose,
Which left him sleepy and ready to doze.

He curled inside his spiral shell,
And into a deep sleep he soon fell.
Dreaming of what next he could draw,
Omalvus began to quietly snore.

A few hours later when Omalvus awoke,
The sight he saw nearly made him choke.
His picture was not how he'd left it before;
It was now nothing more than an ugly eyesore.

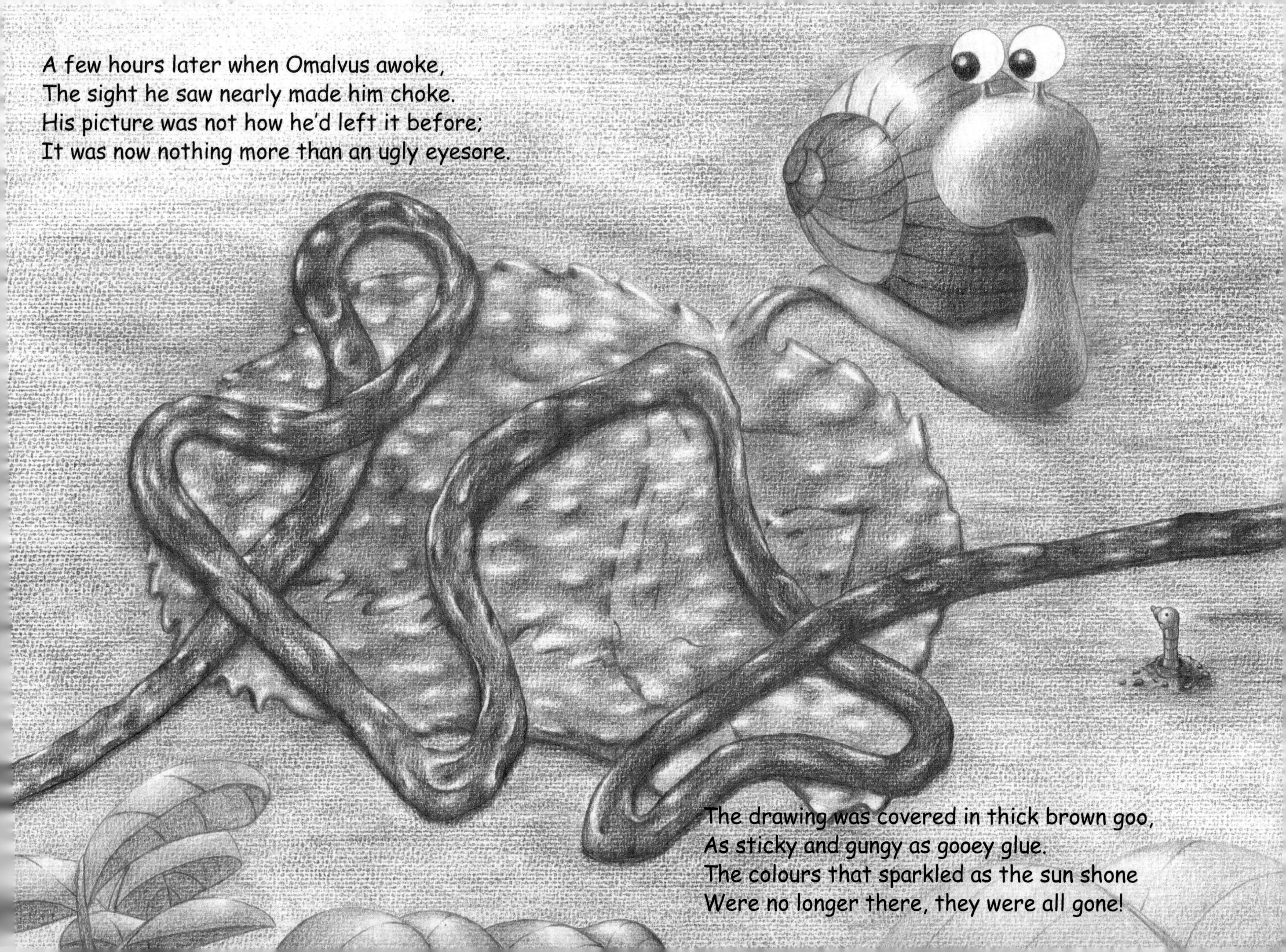

The drawing was covered in thick brown goo,
As sticky and gungy as gooey glue.
The colours that sparkled as the sun shone
Were no longer there, they were all gone!

Omalvus was sad to see such a mess,
How this had happened he couldn't guess.
He wanted to be away from this place,
So off he crawled with a gloomy face.

Past the big cat who was still asleep,
And into the bushes the snail did creep.
To cheer himself up he knew what he'd do:
Tomorrow he'd draw something bright and new.

The next day was sunny, not a cloud in sight,
Omalvus ate leaves in the morning light.
He took a bite and looked at the sky,
Where he saw a bright creature flutter by.

It landed on a flower above his head,
Gently, its four big wings spread.
Purple, orange, red, white and green,
The loveliest butterfly he'd ever seen!

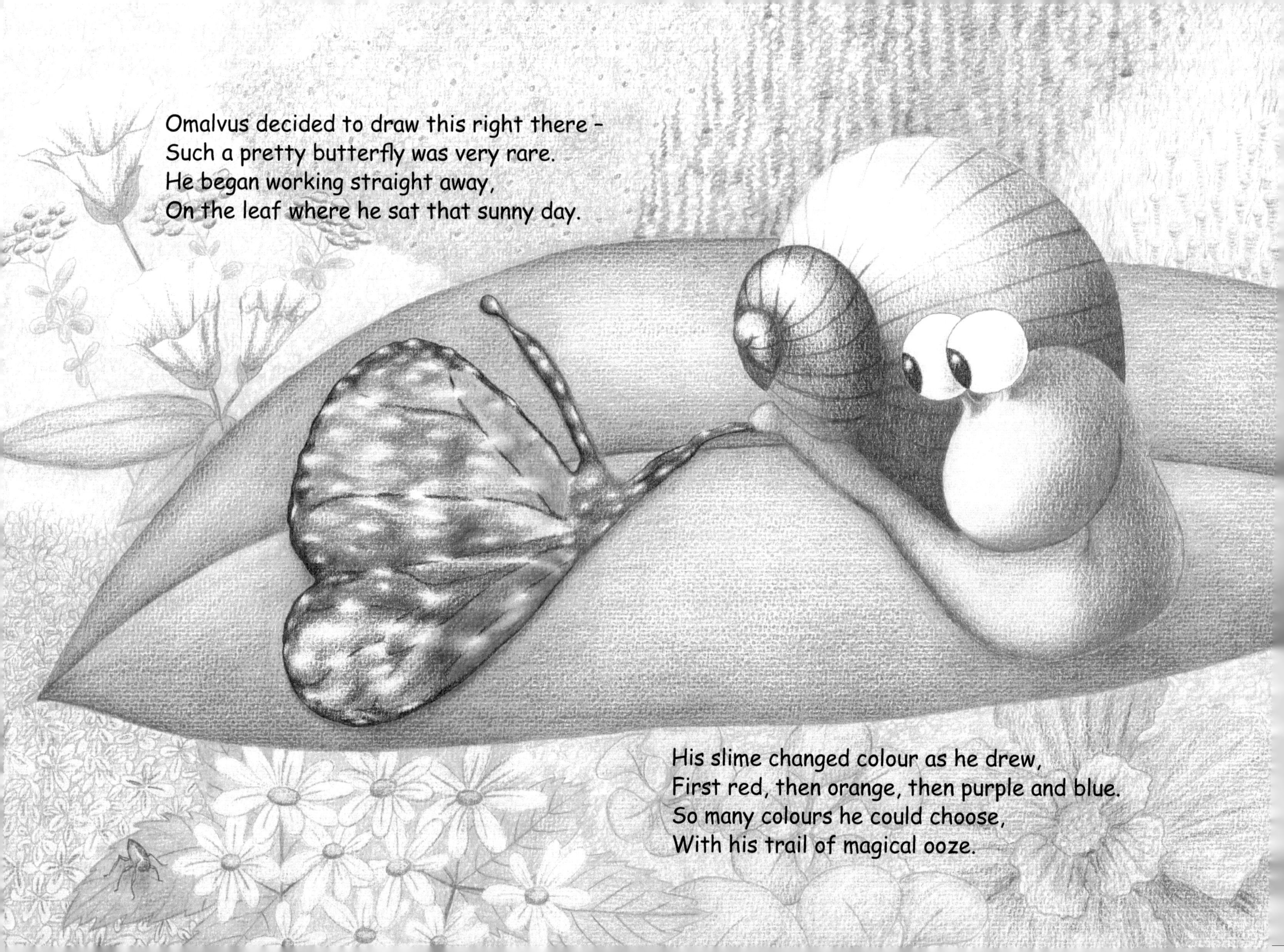

Omalvus decided to draw this right there –
Such a pretty butterfly was very rare.
He began working straight away,
On the leaf where he sat that sunny day.

His slime changed colour as he drew,
First red, then orange, then purple and blue.
So many colours he could choose,
With his trail of magical ooze.

Sometime later that bright day,
The butterfly chose to fly away.
This was no problem for the snail,
He had just finished the last detail.

Of all the pictures he'd ever done,
This really was the best one.
Pleased now that it was complete,
He was happy, hungry and ready to eat.

The nicest leaves were not nearby,
But the tips of plants, way up high.
He really loved to feast on them,
So up he went, along a stem.

He munched, crunched, chomped and chewed,
This really was delicious food.
He ate many leaves then had to stop,
He was so full he thought he'd pop!

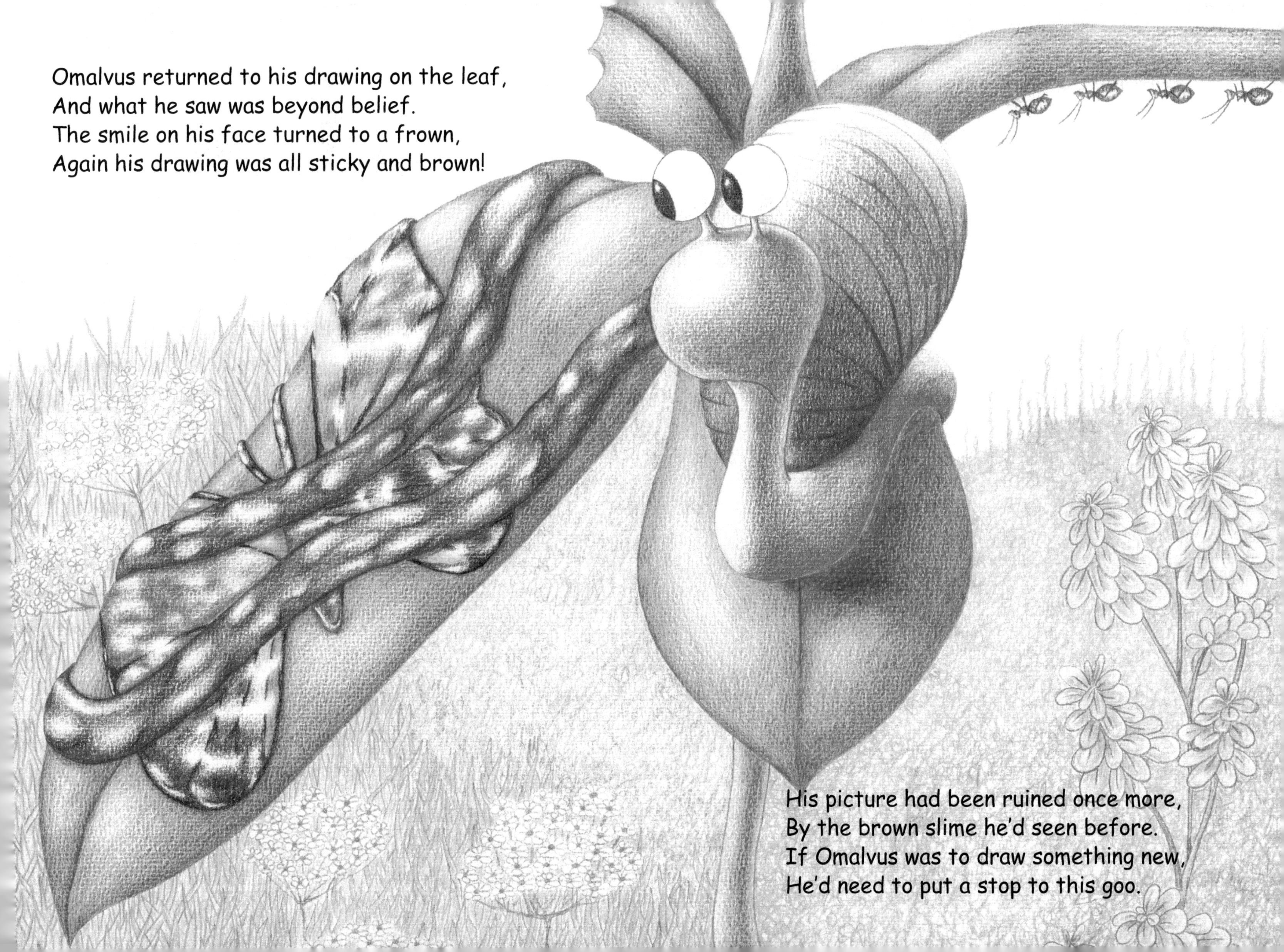

Omalvus returned to his drawing on the leaf,
And what he saw was beyond belief.
The smile on his face turned to a frown,
Again his drawing was all sticky and brown!

His picture had been ruined once more,
By the brown slime he'd seen before.
If Omalvus was to draw something new,
He'd need to put a stop to this goo.

Omalvus awoke early the next day,
And began drawing straight away.
He drew with speed and within nine hours
The snail had drawn some pretty white flowers.

Then Omalvus went and hid,
Behind a nearby stone he slid.
He hoped to see how the brown slime
Might ruin his work for the third time.

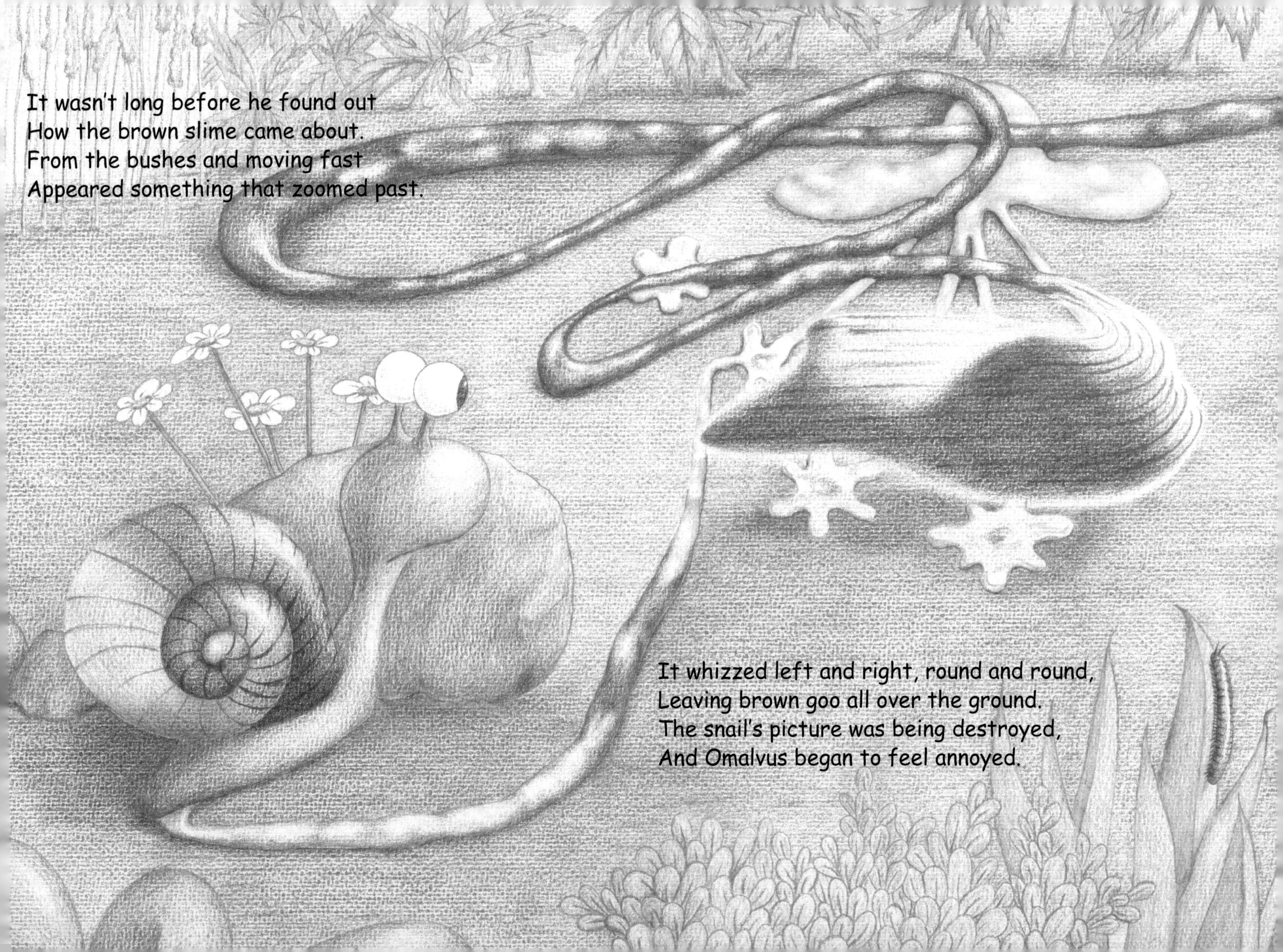

It wasn't long before he found out
How the brown slime came about.
From the bushes and moving fast
Appeared something that zoomed past.

It whizzed left and right, round and round,
Leaving brown goo all over the ground.
The snail's picture was being destroyed,
And Omalvus began to feel annoyed.

Omalvus slid forward and shouted, "No!
Get away from here! Stop doing that! Go!"
The thing was startled and stopped on the spot,
And a huge surprise Omalvus got.

He had wondered what the thing might be,
Now here it was for him to see.
If he'd tried to guess he'd surely fail,
He never imagined it could be a snail!

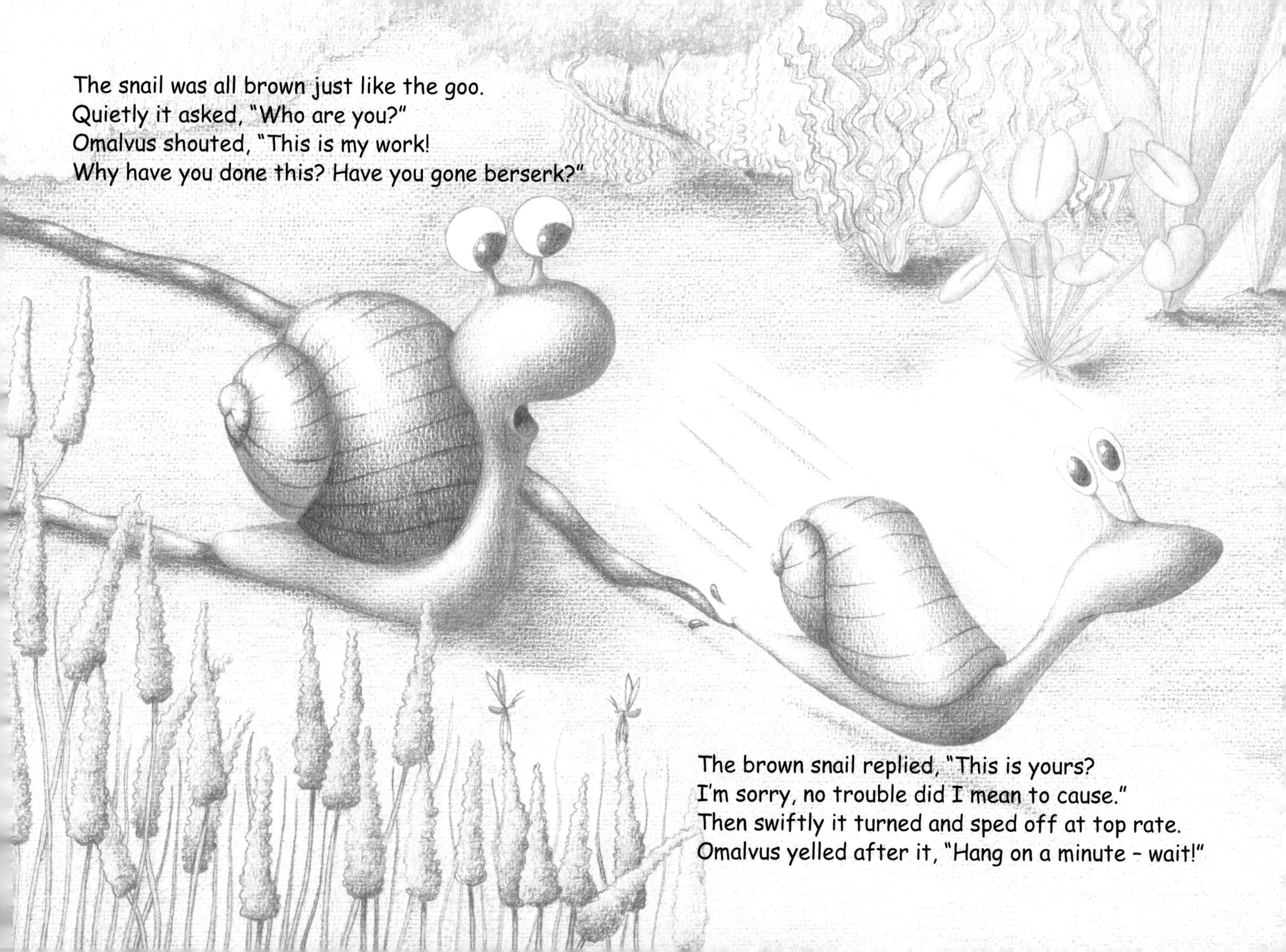

The snail was all brown just like the goo.
Quietly it asked, "Who are you?"
Omalvus shouted, "This is my work!
Why have you done this? Have you gone berserk?"

The brown snail replied, "This is yours?
I'm sorry, no trouble did I mean to cause."
Then swiftly it turned and sped off at top rate.
Omalvus yelled after it, "Hang on a minute – wait!"

Such a fast snail he'd never before seen,
To know how it did this he was very keen.
He wished that he could move this quick,
So decided to have a go at the trick.

He tried to zoom from here to there,
From there to here, to anywhere.
Sometime later he stopped and sighed,
It was impossible, however he tried.

The following day was rainy and grey,
So anything he drew just got washed away.
Today was a good day to eat and eat,
For the rain made leaves so juicy and sweet.

Omalvus was chewing when he heard a whoosh –
The noise seemed to come from a nearby bush.
From leaf to leaf something zipped for a munch –
It was the brown snail enjoying some lunch!

Omalvus shouted, "Hey there! Yoo-hoo!
Come over here, I want a word with you."
The brown snail stared, unsure what to do,
Then it raced over in a second or two.

"Hello there," it said. "Sharla is my name.
Sorry about your work, I am the one to blame.
Those wonderful colours make me feel quite mad.
I'm plain and brown, which makes me sad."

The things she'd said left him quite amazed,
Lost for words he simply gazed.
"Why are you staring?" Sharla said.
"If you want to yell, just go ahead."

"I'm sorry," said Omalvus, "I don't mean to stare,
But there is something of which you're unaware.
Thinking you're plain is such a pity,
Because in fact you are very pretty."

"Nonsense," Sharla said. "I don't believe you.
Brown things aren't pretty, it's simply not true."
"I think you're wrong," he said. "There's lots about.
Just look around if you are in doubt."

"Where?" she said. "What brown things are nice?"
"You," he said, "rabbits, caterpillars and mice,
Millipedes, moths, mushrooms, turtles and toads,
Hedgehogs and birds. I can think of loads!"

"Ants, acorns, squirrels and tree bark.
There are many more," he said, "I could go on till dark!"
"OK, I believe you!" Sharla exclaimed.
"How silly I've been, I'm so ashamed.

"You've helped me see sense, I must thank you.
Is there anything I can do to make it up to you?"
"I know," Omalvus said, "tell me about your gift.
How do you crawl so fast and so swift?"

"What do you mean? Aren't all snails like me?"
"No they're not," he replied, "but I'd sure like to be.
You move so quick with grace and ease –
How do you do it? Will you show me, please?"

"I wish I could," Sharla said, "but I haven't got a clue;
It's just something I naturally do."
"Oh well, never mind," he said. "I can't do it, I've tried."
"Hop on my shell," she said. "I'll give you a ride!"

They whizzed through the garden, past the big pond,
Under a hedge to the garden beyond.
They sped through this garden he'd never before been,
And Omalvus saw things he'd never before seen.

They passed a spider whose web had a gap,
So they whooshed through his tatty flytrap!
Omalvus was amazed at the wonders they passed,
He'd never travelled so far and never so fast.

The rain now slowed, but on they sped.
Where they were going, Sharla hadn't said.
She stopped on a tree stump high above the ground,
And said, "Look at the view, you can see all around."

Omalvus gazed at the beautiful sight.
The rain now stopped, it was getting bright.
He looked to the sky and saw a rainbow –
He wanted to draw this and the view below.

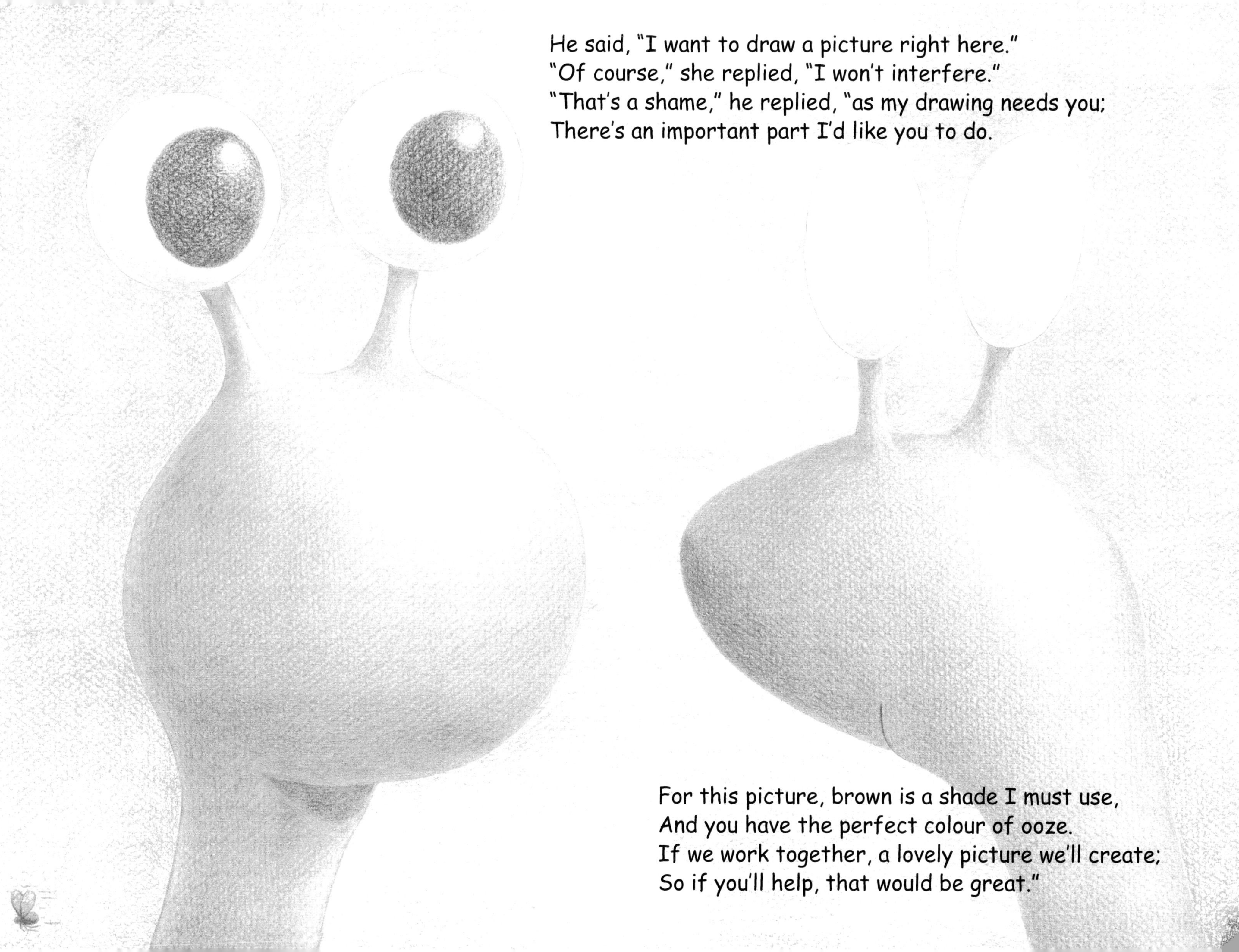

He said, "I want to draw a picture right here."
"Of course," she replied, "I won't interfere."
"That's a shame," he replied, "as my drawing needs you;
There's an important part I'd like you to do.

For this picture, brown is a shade I must use,
And you have the perfect colour of ooze.
If we work together, a lovely picture we'll create;
So if you'll help, that would be great."

Sharla said, "I'd love to, but what do I do?
I don't know how to draw, I haven't a clue."
"It's easy," he said. "I'll draw the outline;
You'll see where to colour, you'll do just fine."

Sharla watched Omalvus while he drew,
Then speedily she coloured with her goo.
"Is this OK?" she said. "Am I doing it right?"
"Amazing!" Omalvus replied with great delight.

They finished their drawing as the sun set,
Their coloured slime sparkled, still sticky and wet.
The picture was wonderful they both agreed.
"Beautiful!" Omalvus said. "The best ever indeed!"

"What fun we've had," she said. "I'm so glad we met;
This is a day I'll never forget."
"Me too," said Omalvus. "Let's do it again soon.
In fact, how about tonight? By the light of the moon!"

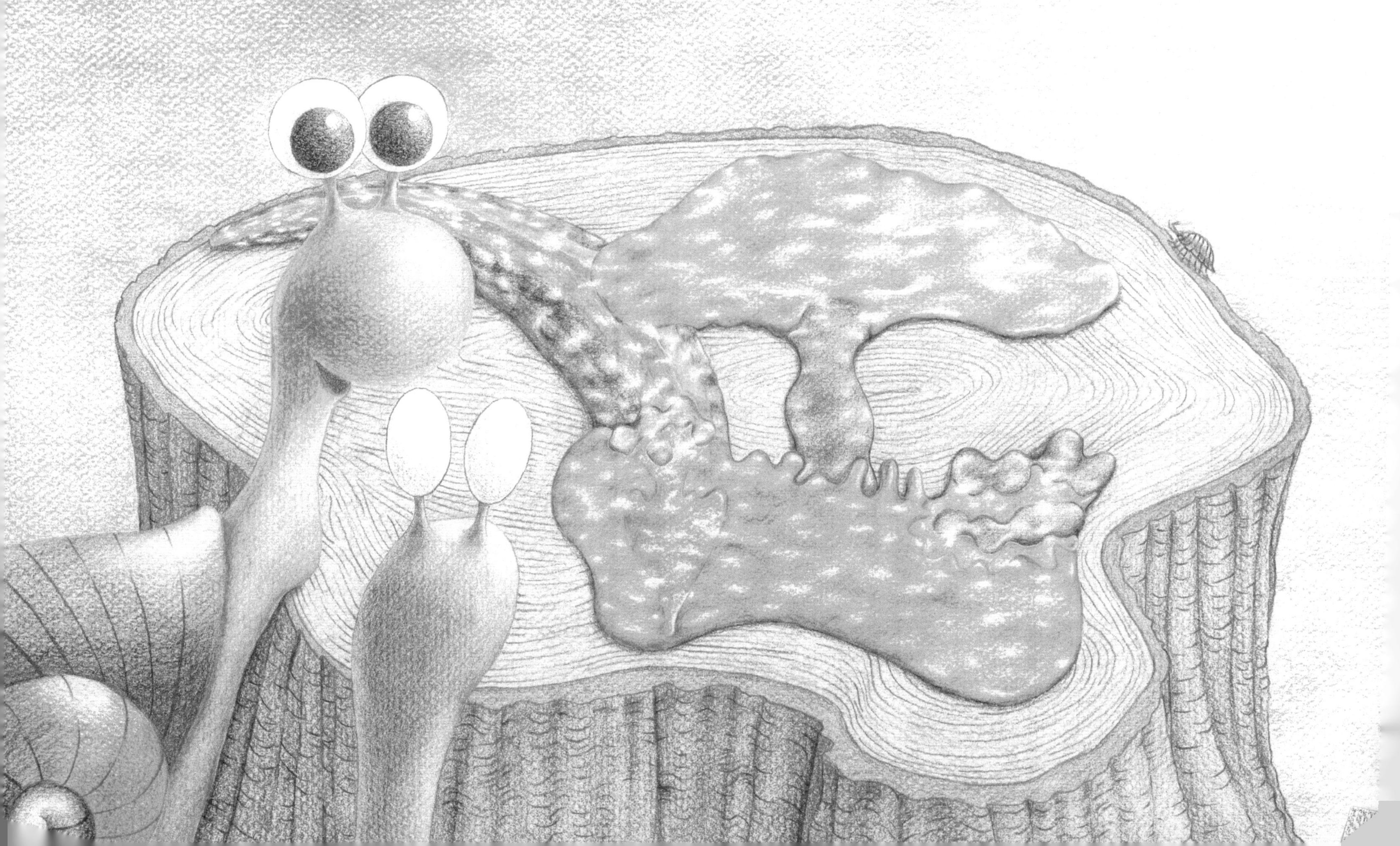

That evening in the moonlight they drew a night scene,
Their coloured slime sparkled with a beautiful sheen.
The following day they spent in just the same way,
And from then on they were together every single day.

On that first day a great friendship had begun,
Adventures they'd have, full of thrills and fun.
Sharla carried them to places to explore;
Together they drew all the wonders they saw.

So if one day you see two snails somewhere,
Take a close look, but quietly and with care.
If you scare them they may zoom away in a flash,
Perhaps leaving an oozy brown trail as they dash.

But if luck is with you at this time,
You may see a picture drawn in slime.
This could be the work of two special snails,
Omalvus and Sharla, and their amazing slime trails!

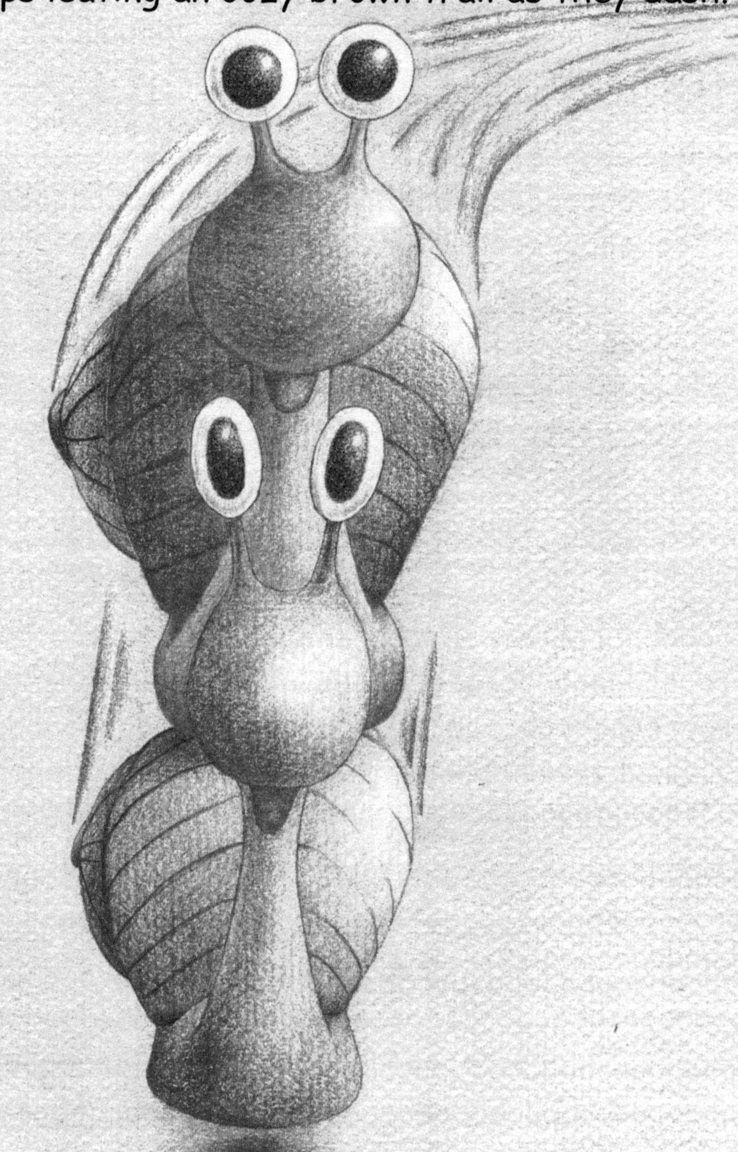